MIND YOUR MANNERS!

DIANE GOODE

FARRAR STRAUS GIROUX • NEW YORK

...to dine with the Abbotts...

...always remember to...

...mind your manners!

Come not to the table without having your hands
and face washed, and your head combed.

Sit not down till thou art bidden by thy parents or superiors.

Be sure thou sittest down in thy due place.

Be not the first that begins to eat.

Bend thy body a little downward to thy plate,
when thou movest any thing to thy mouth.

Make not a noise with thy tongue, mouth, lips or breath, in eating or drinking.

Find no fault with any thing that is given thee.

Throw not any thing under the table.

Look not earnestly on any one that is eating.

Spit not, cough not, nor blow thy nose at the table, if it may be avoided;
but if there be necessity, do it aside and without much noise.

Bite not thy bread, but break it.

Blow not thy meat, but with patience wait until it be cool.

Offer not to carve for thyself, or to take any thing,
though it be that which thou dost greatly desire.

Smell not of thy meat, nor put it to thy nose.

Hold not thy knife upright in thy hand, but sloping.

Gnaw not bones at the table.

Greese not thy fingers or napkin more than necessity requires.

Pick not thy teeth at the table, unless holding thy napkin
before thy mouth with thine other hand.

Lean not thy elbow on the table, nor on the back of thy chair.

Foul not the napkin all over but at one corner.

If thy superiors be discoursing, meddle not with the matter;
but be silent, except thou art spoken unto.

Drink not, nor speak with any thing in thy mouth.

Stare not in the face of any one (especially thy superiors)
nor fix thine eye upon the plate of another.

Foul not the table-cloth.

Spit not fourth any thing that is not convenient to be swallowed, as the stones of plumbs, cherries or such like; but with thy left hand neatly remove them to the side of thy plate.

Eat not too much, but moderately.

Stuff not thy mouth so as to fill thy cheeks; be content with smaller mouthfuls.

Frown not, nor murmur if there be any thing at the table which thy parents or
strangers with them eat of, whilst thou hast none given thee.

Eat not too fast, or with greedy behaviour.

Put not a bit into thy mouth till the former be swallowed.

As soon as thou shalt be moderately satisfied; or whenever thy parents bid thee, rise up from the table, though thy superiors sit still.

When thanks are to be returned after eating return to thy place, and stand reverently, till it be done; then with a bow withdraw out of the room, unless thou art bidden to stay...

...And hope that the next time...

...the Abbotts remember to mind their manners.

AUTHOR'S NOTE

Not long ago, my husband gave me a spelling book he found in an antique shop. The book measured only four by five inches, just big enough to fit comfortably into a child's pocket. The pages were bound up with long stitches and never had endpapers or board.

Published in Connecticut in 1802 (fourth edition), the title boasted that the book was "calculated to render reading completely easy to little children" and to "impress upon their minds the importance of religion, and the advantages of good manners." This intrigued me. What were children learning during the Federal period when our nation was making the transition from the Colonies to a free nation? I turned the thin pages until I came to lesson III, the section on table manners. The rules for behavior at the table were listed with straightforward simplicity. As I read them, my mind immediately formed pictures. If children needed to be told not to "spit at the table," then obviously children—and adults—were spitting at the table, and much more!

But who were these people? What did they eat and wear and how did they conduct themselves? I was inspired to learn more about the history of etiquette and of childhood in America. My hope is that some young readers will also ask questions about the life of their forefathers. I think they will discover that our American manners, whether you love them or hate them, spring from a love of freedom and equality. And if our manners are not perfect, then let it be said that we are still learning.

For the purpose of my book, I had to edit the original rules for behavior at the table, but they follow here in their entirety.

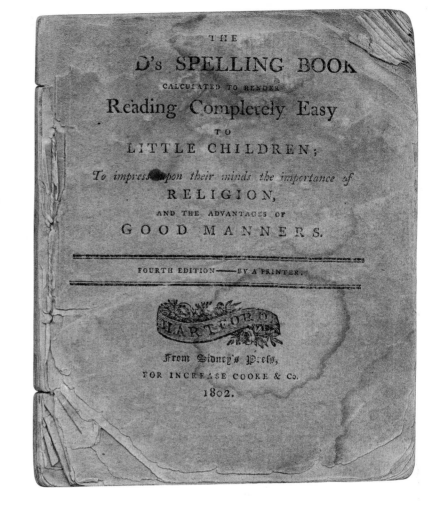

Lesson III. Of children's behaviour at table.

1 Come not to the table without having your hands and face washed, and your head combed.

2 Sit not down till thou art bidden by thy parents or superiors.

3 Be sure thou never sittest down till a blessing be desired, and then in thy due place.

4 Offer not to carve for thyself, or to take any thing, though it be that which thou dost greatly desire.

5 Find no fault with any thing that is given thee.

6 When thou hast meat given thee, be not the first that begins to eat.

7 Speak not at the table; if thy superiors be discoursing, meddle not with the matter; but be silent, except thou art spoken unto.

8 Eat not too fast, or with greedy behaviour.

9 Eat not too much, but moderately.

10 Make not a noise with thy tongue, mouth, lips or breath, in eating or drinking.

11 Stare not in the face of any one (especially thy superiors) at the table; nor fix thine eye upon the plate of another, nor upon the meat on the table.

12 Greese not thy fingers or napkin more than necessity requires.

13 Bite not thy bread, but break it; but not with slovenly fingers, nor with the same wherewith thou takest up thy meat.

14 Take not salt with a greasy knife.

15 Spit not, cough not, nor blow thy nose at the table, if it may be avoided; but if there be necessity, do it aside and without much noise.

16 Lean not thy elbow on the table, nor on the back of thy chair.

17 Stuff not thy mouth so as to fill thy cheeks; be content with smaller mouthfuls.

18 Blow not thy meat, but with patience wait until it be cool.

19 Smell not of thy meat, nor put it to thy nose; turn it not the other side upward to view it upon thy plate.

20 Throw not any thing under the table.

21 Hold not thy knife upright in thy hand, but sloping; and lay it down at thy right hand, with the blade upon thy plate.

22 Spit not fourth any thing that is not convenient to be swallowed, as the stones of plumbs, cherries or such like; but with thy left hand neatly remove them to the side of thy plate.

23 Bend thy body a little downward to thy plate, when thou movest any thing that is sauced to thy mouth.

24 Look not earnestly on any one that is eating.

25 Foul not the table-cloth.

26 Foul not the napkin all over but at one corner.

27 Gnaw not bones at the table, but clean them with thy knife (unless they be very small ones) and hold them not with a whole hand, but with two fingers.

28 Drink not, nor speak with any thing in thy mouth.

29 Put not a bit into thy mouth till the former be swallowed.

30 Before and after thou drinkest, wipe thy lips with a napkin.

31 Pick not thy teeth at the table, unless holding thy napkin before thy mouth with thine other hand.

32 Drink not till thou hast emptied thy mouth.

33 Frown not, nor murmur if there be any thing at the table which thy parents or strangers with them eat of, whilst thou hast none given thee.

34 As soon as thou shalt be moderately satisfied; or whenever thy parents bid thee, rise up from the table, though others thy superiors sit still.

35 When thanks are to be returned after eating return to thy place, and stand reverently, till it be done; then with a bow withdraw out of the room, unless thou art bidden to stay.

For Peter

Distributed in Canada by Douglas & McIntyre Publishing Group
Printed and bound in China by South China Printing Co. Ltd.
Designed by Jay Colvin
First edition, 2005
1 3 5 7 9 10 8 6 4 2

www.fsgkidsbooks.com

Library of Congress Cataloging-in-Publication Data
Goode, Diane.
    Mind your manners! / Diane Goode.— 1st ed.
        p.   cm.
    ISBN-13: 978-0-374-34975-2
    ISBN-10: 0-374-34975-4
    1. Etiquette for children and teenagers.   I. Title.

BJ1857.C5G66 2005
395.1'22—dc22
                                                    2004047179